AF440885

Last Ride of the
Season

Last Ride of the Season

Stories

Daniel Kinsley

SIDE A

Howl…
Excerpt from "The Guide to Making a
Mixtape"…
Speaking Terms…
You Can't Kiss Every Girl…
The God of Small Things…

SIDE B

Enchanted Rock…
Living Room Karaoke…
Cloak and Dagger…
Haunted…
Last Ride of the Season…

SIDE A

Disquiet & Desire

HOWL

It begins with a guy who is sitting at a bar, picking at a napkin.

He is meant to be on a first date, but it is five minutes past the scheduled time, and he is alone. He is debating whether he should send a text, but it feels too soon. Another guy comes over to ask if the seat next to him is taken. He says yes, he's waiting for someone—I think. This last part he adds without meaning to. The other guy laughs and says, first date? Yes, he tells him. Right on, man, good luck. The other guy moves away.

More minutes pass, and still no word. He is beginning to think that he's been stood up, and finds that he is not all that upset. The date in question had been rescheduled twice, and he only agreed to follow through out of a sense of obligation. He is not getting any younger, but he often wrestles with the impulse to just sit at home. It has begun to feel like work to take hold of this feeling. He tells himself that stability is good, better even, and over time, he has lost his appetite for the unexpected.

His thoughts are interrupted by the same guy from before, who asks him if his date is still coming. No, he admits, I don't think so. The seat is all yours. The guy laughs genially. Well, hey man, we're here to play trivia, if you'd like to come join us. We can always use another brain. Okay, he says, sure.

So they walk to the other side of the room, and there is a group of them, six or seven in all, names he only remembers for as long as it takes to hear the next one. There is an energy about them, a looseness that he decides immediately he wants to be a part of. He accepts a seat and the guy who recruited him heads back to the bar for another round. There is a woman sitting on the other side of the table, not directly across from him, but one person over.

Hey, she says.

Hi, he says back.

What happened to your date?

I guess I got stood up, he says, laughing as he does, as if it's only just occurred to him.

Trivia is more fun anyway, she says.

Is it? He asks, because something in her tone sounds as if she does not quite believe it.

She laughs and says, it is if you drink enough.

Her eyes linger on him a moment, and her gaze feels intense, as if she can see exactly what he is thinking. He finds himself wanting to shy away from it, not because he does not like it, but because he does.

The group plays trivia and they are pretty good. There is a heated exchange about the difference between a state slogan and a motto, and the table is split on whether a person can get carpal tunnel in their ankles, but even these mini-arguments are mostly good natured, the kind of banter that only passes between people who know one another very well, as if things could at any moment pass over into something white hot and personal, but they never do, because someone always knows when to let up.

He contributes a few answers to the group with a conviction he does not necessarily believe, but he feels good when they clap his back or reach out for high-fives. They come in second place and cheer as if they have accomplished something much worthier than twenty dollars in bar bucks, but he finds their enthusiasm infectious, and he cheers along with them.

He has had several drinks by now, his missing date long forgotten. He pushes his chair back and asks the man next to him (Dave, he thinks) where the bathroom is.

When he makes his way back toward the bar, he sees

the woman from the table, the one with the strong gaze and she fixes him with it when she says, hey again.

We've got to stop meeting like this, he says, and then immediately wonders why he said it.

He is about to attempt an explanation before she laughs, and the warmth of it brings him out of his head long enough to forget it, smiling instead, as if this was the intended goal all along: to elicit the beautiful sound of her laughter.

I told you trivia was more fun, she says, and he has forgotten their earlier exchange, but agrees anyway, because he is having fun. He wants to say more, but there is no time because she is grabbing his arm and steering him back toward her friends. Come on, she says. There is nothing especially romantic about the gesture, but he relishes how nice it feels to be touched.

The guy who recruited him hands him a celebratory beer and he accepts it with only a hint of reluctance, knowing he will regret it come morning. Fuck it, he decides. This is exactly the sort of spontaneous decision making he is always telling himself he should make more room for. He does not really know these people, but he feels good around them. He begins to catch a few of their names again, recommitting them to memory.

Before long, the bar is beginning to clear out, the trivia crowd and the happy hour drinkers heading for the doors as the sun begins to set. Someone says hey man, we're going back to Johnny's roof to hang, are you coming? He looks around, hoping to catch the eye of his mystery girl, hoping to get some sign, but she is speaking to someone else, her back turned. Yeah, he says, that sounds great.

The guy who recruited him is settling a tab at the bar and he says, hey let me give you some cash, but the man waves him away, says, your money is no good here. The guy seems sober enough to be sincere, and he is touched by this small kindness, and if he is honest, a little envious of the guy's confidence.

He follows the group outside and they say come on, Dave doesn't drink and we can all fit in his truck. He starts to explain that he drove himself before realizing he is too drunk to drive, so instead he says okay, putting off any concerns about how he will get his car home until later.

He hops into the bed of a new pickup with a few of the others and settles in, smiling to himself, wishing for a moment that he had a mirror to wink at.

He looks up in time to see his girl on the way to the cab of the truck, and feels a hit of disappointment that she will not be joining them in the back.

Impulsively he calls to her, asks her name. He is not sure if he never got it, or if he just can't remember. She says something but he doesn't catch it, drowned out by the truck coming to life. He must make a face because she laughs, then winks and cocks a finger gun at his chest. He clutches his heart and leans back, a direct hit.

She is turning then, and he can't be sure, but he thinks he sees her laugh. When they get to the roof, he decides he will not shy away from her gaze. If he is given the chance, he will stand up to the moment.

Then the truck is moving, and the air is warm, and they can't be moving faster than thirty-five miles per hour, but in a way it feels like they are flying, and it is both exhilarating and a little terrifying.

Beside him, someone lets out a howl, a sound so pure and filled with joy that he joins in, echoing the sound until each of them is taking a turn, their voices overlapping. It has been years since he last felt this way, and it occurs to him that maybe the bar was actually a portal, and he has stepped into the past, to a time when his potential seemed as limitless as life's possibilities, just a series of infinite hypotheticals.

He feels a swell of emotion, feels it building to a song that seems like it might burst from his skin. Once, I was untouched, he thinks. There was no right or wrong path, no path at all, just a series of choices that might lead anywhere. The world was whatever you wanted it to be, whatever you made it, and maybe those things can still be true.

He wants to shout over the wind and tell everyone how he feels, but he is not sure how, does not know where to find the words, if they even exist.

Someone calls his name, and he howls in response, and the moment has not yet passed as a chorus of cheers rise to meet him.

EXCERPT FROM "THE GUIDE TO
MAKING A MIXTAPE"

The art of making a mixtape is a delicate one.
Of course, it should be noted for posterity that no one actually uses tapes anymore. Readers of a certain age may already be scratching their heads, but alas, for a certain type of person, this term remains firmly and immovably in the vernacular. "Hey, I made you a mix CD," or more likely, "Hey I made you a Spotify playlist," lacks a certain poetry (even if it remains technically correct). It fails to convey the care and thought that went into its construction. A great mix has a certain flow to it, each song knowing its place. In this way, it is no different than a great record by a single artist. Think of the greatest albums in recorded history; there is a symmetry present that makes it feel as if each piece fits in such a way that it simply couldn't be any other way and remain as essential.
Ideally, whether you are playing it safe or genre-swapping like a particularly adventurous chef, there is a sonic consistency that ties your ingredients together. People love to hit the shuffle button these days (including the author of this text), but there was a time when you couldn't do that! A record had a story to tell, and you had to experience the narrative the way the artist intended, with a clear beginning, middle, and end. Tracks could be skipped, but you might risk missing a vital piece of the story. And make no mistake, a great mixtape *is* a story, and it will have something of a three act structure (or perhaps, dear reader, you or someone you are acquainted with is confident and skilled enough to break the rules; a George Saunders style mix-master, if you will) but

even those who are brave or skilled enough to break the rules are ultimately after the same thing: *they are trying to say something!*

Using someone else's poetry to express how you feel can be a particularly effective example of the death of the author; some of the greatest break up songs are probably about a guy who is struggling to quit smoking. But that's okay, because the best songwriters are able to take something that's very personal to them and make it feel like it was written just for you. Making someone a mixtape is a lot like that, except without nearly as much heavy lifting.

What is most important, however, is this: a truly great mixtape should tell the other person something that you wouldn't be able to tell them in any other way. It doesn't matter if it's a secret, a word of encouragement, a confession, or a joke. *That* is what the music is for: to give voice to the ineffable.

Now, you always run the risk that this person will interpret a song differently than you may have intended, or perhaps they will miss that one line that you really wanted them to hear, the one that justifies the inclusion of the whole song. A great listener will give you an edge because ideally they will be putting as much effort into the dissection of what you are trying to say as you did in deciding how to say it. And sure, sometimes it's obvious, but that doesn't matter. A compelling story doesn't always have to be complicated to resonate; there's a reason people still go crazy for The Beatles' early stuff.

On the other hand, there is subtext to consider. It's inevitable, but maybe not always intentional.

For instance, if you're working on something meant to be played at a loud volume with the windows down while on your way to the Jersey shore, you probably don't need someone to tell you why the inclusion of "Thunder Road" is both perfectly apropos and also doesn't engender much of a deeper reading.

Let's say, however, that you're working on a project

for your crush. Well, then suddenly subtext becomes *very* important. It can be an effective (and sometimes subtle) way of letting someone know you are thinking of them, but even more than that, the way it's received might reveal some deeper truth about what this person believes you feel about them, or whether they might feel the same way.

In a perfect world, this person would make you a tape, thereby creating a dialogue with your songs; blending together to form a labyrinth that reveals something deep and true about its architect, the sort of thing that is too hard to say aloud but needs to be shared nonetheless.

Now that we've talked a bit about the how, hopefully by this time you've been able to start forming some general ideas. In the next several chapters, we will be getting into more specific archetypes you can rely upon. On the next page are several examples to give you an idea of what sorts of things you might like to start thinking about.

(Ed. Note: We have a whole chapter dedicated to each of the below categories [see table of contents] but in the interest of brevity, this is meant to act only as an introduction to several of the most popular choices).

THE LOVE SONG: You may find yourself in a blossoming romance and want to express a sudden infusion of joy and optimism, or perhaps you find yourself in a more complicated situation where you aren't sure how the other person feels, or maybe *they* aren't sure how they feel! It could be a declaration of love already well-known, or part of a grand effort to save a failing affair. Hell, there are love songs about inanimate objects, plants and pets; sex, drugs and rock 'n roll, or any other thing you can imagine! There are more things in Heaven and Earth, like the man said. It is estimated that more songs have been written about love than any other subject, so whatever your heart is going through, whether high or low, loving yourself or someone else, the love song is a reliable staple that can be slotted in comfortably on nearly any occasion.

THE SAD SONG: Similarly to the love song, there are near infinite variations on this theme. Our capacity for sadness mirrors our capacity for love, and there are sad songs for just about every occasion. Did you lose a loved one? Have your heart broken? Have a bad day? (See: "Keep Me In Your Heart"; "My Backwards Walk"; "I Don't Like Mondays"). Perhaps the occasion is more bittersweet, like when the last echoes of heartbreak fade, or that unique period when you are adjusting to the growing pains of being a young adult. Whatever the cause for the listener's grief, there is a song that will remind them they are not alone.

THE ENERGIZER: The energizer makes for a great opening track! This is a feet-stomping, earth-quaking, booty-shaking, fist-pumping song that makes you want to shout, dance, or get moving. They can run the gamut from inspirational hype for cardio activity ("Eye of the Tiger") to the full recovery of a broken heart or an addiction ("Return of the Mack"; "I'm Still Standing"). Whether it stems from excitement, motivation, or even frustration (!) the primary criteria for the energizer is to get the listener's blood pumping.

THE CLOSING SONG: This is a chance to sum up what you are using your mixtape to say. Where does the story end? Is it triumphant or tragic or somewhere in between? Does it go out with a bang? A big finish, for instance, accompanied by a bruising chorus and deafening instruments, or is it something more contemplative? Acoustic guitars and harmonicas, maybe. Perhaps a blend of the two, like the rock ballads popularized by heavy metal hair bands. The trick is to find a song that will leave the listener with whatever impression you've been trying to convey the whole time, which may seem like a lot to ask of a single song, but it's important to remember that because of the way our brains are wired, we tend to remember how we felt at the end of things.

For instance, you may be thinking of a song right now, a song that means something special to you. Maybe it was a song someone gave to you on a mixtape! You'll likely be thinking of how that song makes you feel now, or perhaps the way you felt the first time you heard it. You may be considering who you were then, what kind of memories are attached to that song, the places you've been and the people you were there with.

You may be thinking of the way your friends belted out the hook together, or the way it took on a different meaning after your lover was gone. Or maybe you are thinking of a time when a song reminded you that everything was really truly going to be okay.

A mixtape may seem like a small thing, but it isn't. A great mixtape can feel like a miracle.

SPEAKING TERMS

When it finally happens, you are caught totally off guard.

By all accounts, you shouldn't be—it's been coming for awhile now, in that inexorable way that disaster always does—if only you had cared to pay attention. No, that isn't exactly fair; you've been paying plenty of attention, but that isn't the same as doing anything about it.

Still, you've been down this road before, on so many practice runs; the familiarity just means it's become part of the routine. After so many dress rehearsals, you had nearly fooled yourself into believing this day would never actually arrive.

You say the same things, and so does your lover, but something feels different. They tell you that it's over, that they really mean it this time. They just don't see you being forever. You say okay, but secretly you believe this might still be like the other times. It takes you a few days to realize what was different: there was no sense of passion to the proceedings. No, suddenly, it was as if they had grown very tired.

This is the moment you know that it's really over.

Of course, you will convince yourself a little longer that there is hope (and you will hate yourself for it, just a bit) but it's what we do when we are afraid. It's a survival mechanism; being angry at yourself for wanting to believe that this person still loves you is like being angry at your stomach for growling to be fed. We may be able to survive longer without love, but as far as it goes, it is just as essential.

You say you won't write, but you do. You draft long, meandering texts, emails filled with so many words, words, words, all of it to say the same thing: don't go.

You say you won't call, but of course, you do. Only when you have had far too much to drink to say anything sensible, but these are the only circumstances in which you feel brave, or perhaps foolish enough, to reach for your phone.

Eventually, they will tire of this game. It's over, they will remind you. I'm sorry. Please, it's time to move on.

You will wander through days, then weeks, thinking you are better off, you are free, it was never going to work anyway, before remembering that this isn't how you feel at all. The intensity of your longing will be unbearable, and you will feel shame at both your hubris and your desire.

You will call loved ones and try to explain where it hurts, as if there is any way to quantify such a loss. You will listen to their advice, to their consolation, to their loving silence, all of which is well meant but ultimately toothless against your grief.

For another few weeks, your apartment will become unlivable. You will sleep on the couch, tossing and aching, but too afraid to return to your bedroom alone. You will take down the photos of happier times, then return them to their proper places, then take them down again.

You will wander through bars and humid city streets in search of something, anything, to earn you a reprieve from feeling like you are unworthy of love, alone because you are broken. The person that you love is out there, surely happier without you. Surely, their life is more fulfilling now. They are having more fun, better sex, less trouble without you.

Eventually, you will begin dating again. Mostly it doesn't make you feel much better, but it usually doesn't make you feel worse. You will meet people you like, whose company you enjoy, but they will not satisfy you. It isn't you, you'll want to tell them. It isn't even as if their crime is not being your lover; it's just that they are strangers and this process makes you so tired.

The first time you have sex with someone else, you

will wish you hadn't. You will still feel this way after the second time, but it will be far less visceral.

You will go on this way for as long as it takes.

One day, you will decide you have had enough of sleeping on the couch, and you will return to your bed. You will have trouble falling asleep, but you will wake up feeling as if maybe you have turned a small corner. You will find reasons to get out of the house that no longer make you feel like you are running from something.

Months will pass, then years. New lovers will come and go. You will change careers, move to another city. Sometimes you will come across old photos on your phone, or hear a song that you both loved and think, huh.

One day, you will reconnect with your former lover on some social media platform. Private messages will be exchanged, and you will speak to one another in a way that is both formal yet familiar. You will update one another on your lives, but only in broad details. You will wonder what they think of you now, if they still think of you at all, if they have any regrets.

Your life together now feels like a dream, something you read in a novel that you only half-remember. You will make promises not to be strangers, to be cordial, now that so much time has passed. In this way, you will be closing a door and keeping a nearby window cracked open.

You will want to say more, but you won't, either out of fear that they won't want to hear it or that they won't feel the same (if there could be said to be much of a difference).

You will part as friends, or at least, something like it, and you will tell yourself that this is all right, that you will not feel anything the next time you stumble onto old photos, or hear that song, the one you both used to love.

You know that real life isn't as neat as the stories we tell ourselves, that this will be the nearest thing you will ever experience to closure, and maybe, maybe it can be enough.

YOU CAN'T KISS EVERY GIRL

I. 2018

He sees her, but she doesn't see him, not at first.

When they walk into the bar, the wandering strobe lights on the ceiling land right on her, just long enough to catch his eye. He and his friends sidle up to the stick and order drinks, but he glances back a few times, checking to see if she's still there.

I'll be right back, he says to the guy standing closest to him. Sensing what's going on, the guy says, hang on, are we hitting on girls? I'm coming with you.

All right, but be cool.

Fuck you, he says, I'm always cool.

There are at least six of them, maybe eight, dancing easily in view of the stage where a DJ spins records.

Hi, he says, when he gets near enough.

Hi back, she says, turning toward him without breaking her rhythm.

I'm Vic, he says. This is Dylan, he's kind of an idiot.

Hey, Dylan says, moving closer to be heard. Who's your friend?

Which one?

The one with the great tits, he says.

Vic looks at her as if to say, I told you, but he is surprised to see her laughing. That's Maddy, she says, she's *very* single.

See you later pal, he says, patting Vic on the shoulder.

Well, he says, after they're alone again.

Don't worry, she's going to eat him alive.

Oh thank god, it's what we all deserve.

Holly, by the way. Are you guys locals?

No, we're in for the weekend. Bachelor party.

Oh, how original, she says, but she's smiling.

Hey, there are worse things to be than unoriginal. What about you?

I'm visiting, too. Some of the girls are local, but the rest of us flew in for a birthday celebration.

Nice, he says. I don't know about you, but I could use another drink. Can I get you something?

Sure, she says.

A few songs later, the bachelors and the birthday girls have merged in that companionable way that people do when everyone is young and drunk and on vacation. By the time someone proposes they move on to another bar, the two groups have become one.

Momentum carries them all of half a block before someone wanders into a honky-tonk, the house band belting out an old rock tune with the kind of energy that makes it sound new. Let's dance, one of the girls says. Half of them take to the floor, while the other half swarm the bar for more courage. Vic hangs back, wanting to see if Holly will come to him, not wanting to force anything that isn't there.

She dances with abandon, her arms and legs and hips moving in fluid unison, her white cotton dress rising from the floor as she spins around. He likes watching her, feels envious of her self-possession. He's not much of a dancer, but he would try if she asked him to.

Eventually, he is pulled onto the floor, and he stays in his comfort zone: enthusiastic if not especially skilled, moving in time with the music in a simple two step. He wants to go to her, but he doesn't, even when he thinks he feels her eyes on him.

The night rolls on, and by closing time, they have run through another round of bars, chasing the booze and the music and the laughs until the lights come on and they are ushered out, told to go home or anyway, someplace else.

Some of them call it a night, but the rest of them splinter off in search of food, finding their way to an all-night diner for chicken and waffles, breakfast that never ends, cups of coffee to take the edge off. The place is jammed with the after-hours crowd, those eager to find any excuse not to give up on the night.

Vic decides not to be so passive this late in the game and makes sure he gets a seat across from Holly. They fill the place with their raucous laughter and he feels sure that it's more than just booze fueling their chemistry.

They might have stayed all night, but once the birthday girl bows out, the domino effect begins as more of the group decides maybe they should quit before the sun rises, after all.

As a matter of chance, they are the last ones out the door after settling up, and they trail their friends down the street, meandering toward home.

Ahead, Dylan and Maddy and a few of the others race to beat the crosswalk signal, leaving the two of them stranded on the opposite side. Sucks to suuuuck, Dylan calls back at them. It isn't very funny, but they're high off the night and still drunk and she turns to him laughing and he leans in to kiss her, but she turns away.

She takes a step back and sits down on the curb, looks up at him. It's very late, she says, and I am very drunk.

I'm sorry, he says, sitting down beside her. I guess I misread the room.

No, look. I like talking to you, but I've got someone at home, so.

He looks down at the hands resting in her lap.

That's okay, we don't have to do anything. I like talking to you, too.

I think that's worse, she says.

He laughs.

How is that worse?

Because you know you can't fuck me, and you still want to hang out.

Don't overcomplicate it, he says.

We might be the only two people still awake, she counters. Our friends have surely abandoned us by now.

First of all, he says. No way that's true. If you really listen, you can hear them—*the creatures of the night!*

You're an idiot, she says.

Anyway, so what if we were?

It's intimate.

He looks up at the sky and the lights and the distant sound of parties that won't quit. Huh, when you put it that way, I guess it is kind of romantic.

She gives him a soft shove.

We should try to catch them, she says. Us girls are supposed to be up early tomorrow.

Okay, he says. You guys are in town for the weekend, right? Maybe we'll see each other again.

Maybe we will, she says.

***

II. 2019

Hi, she says.

Hi, back. It's really good to see you again.

It is, she says.

What?

Well, it's a little crazy isn't it?

I don't know, he says. Is it? I think it's whatever we make of it. You might say it's romantic.

Well, you would, anyway.

Try not to think about it so much, he suggests. Have you eaten yet?

No, and I'm starving.

Well, there's half the problem right there. You're hangry! Come on, the concierge told me there's a killer burger place a few blocks away.

As they walk, he does his best to take her in, to see

how she might have changed in a year. They kept in touch after their trip, but often infrequently, under the safety of exchanging funny memes, or new songs from a band they both liked; whatever subject providing cover for neither to think too hard about what the contact might mean.

When he reached out about being nearby on a work trip, he did so without any confidence at following through, and was relieved when she offered to drive down for a day to catch up, if he was interested.

They are seated in a corner booth at the back of a stylish upscale bar, all paneled oak and expensive leather.

Is this okay?

It's great, she says.

He nods and glances around, taking the place in before his eyes settle on her.

What?

Well, I was thinking your hair looks different. It's lighter, I think.

It is, she says, her hand coming up reflexively. It's my summer look.

Okay, he says, smiling.

What?

No, it's just, it's nice to see you.

You said that already.

Well, it's true. I guess I'm a little nervous, he shrugs. Were you worried at all that this might be awkward?

Were you?

A little, yeah.

And?

I don't think so, do you?

She shakes her head, returns to the menu.

After placing their orders, she says, so, have you talked to her recently?

Nope, he says.

How long?

A little over three months now.

I'm sorry. Are you doing okay?

You know, good days and bad days. How about old what's-his-name? Are you still going strong?

We can't all hop around as easily as you do, she says.

Ouch, he says. I didn't choose the player's life, it chose me.

She cocks her head.

That's one way to say *I'm afraid of intimacy*.

That sort of makes you a perfect fit then, doesn't it?

Ha-ha, she says.

When the food comes, they eat in companionable silence for a while.

So, remind me how long you're in town for?

Just till Wednesday. I'm meant to have a few meetings, then fly home. It's boring mostly, but it passes the time. What about you?

I'll drive back tonight, she says.

He wants to press, but he doesn't. He finds that he wants to ask her about all sorts of things; what is her man like, what does she do with her days? Does she think about the future, and if so, what does she see? But their relationship doesn't make room for those sorts of questions. He knows without having to ask they would only lead to dead ends.

What are you thinking, she says.

It's a beautiful day and we're burning daylight sitting here. How do you feel about taking a walk?

They walk and talk, taking in a city that's largely unfamiliar to them both. He tells her about his new job, and she talks about a new puppy at home, and they ask after one another's friends. They carry on easily enough in this way, even without the booze this time.

What do you think of me, she asks, apropos of nothing.

I think you're smart, and funny and beautiful—

That's very sweet, she says, but that's not exactly what I meant. Let me try again—what do I mean to you? You know, we're here together, and it's, I'm just curious.

That's a big question, he says. I'll answer it, but only under the condition that you'll do the same. Deal?

Deal.

Well, I think when you're young, it feels easy to connect to people, right? You don't really know what you're looking for yet, so you latch onto simple things in a lot of cases. And when you get a little older, you start to realize okay, maybe the real thing is actually a little harder to find. Then if you're lucky, I think the pendulum settles somewhere in the middle. You realize that you'll meet plenty of people who listen to the same music, maybe speak the same strange language that you do, but that doesn't necessarily mean they really understand you. So, you know, I'm not sure how much of that surface level stuff we have, but I do feel like you understand me, and I believe that's pretty rare. When I'm with you, I feel present, you know, and that's not something that comes easily to me. And maybe it's just that we don't know each other that well. Maybe we're only good for short bursts in cities with a warm climate. But even when I wasn't sure if I'd ever see you again, I knew I'd keep thinking about you.

I think I understand what you mean, she says. Full disclosure, I didn't think I'd ever see you again. I've been a flirt my whole life. It's easy, and it can be fun, but it doesn't mean anything. I've never kept in touch with someone the way I did with you. Or really ever thought about them again. And I'll be honest, for a while, it kind of pissed me off. It did! Because who the hell are you? I had a few wild years and they were fun, but that's behind me. My life is good, and my relationship is good, and it's all very tidy. And then here you come out of the clear blue sky and suddenly I'm rethinking all of it. I mean, there's gotta be more to romantic love than commitment, right? Partnering for life just feels so unsustainable. To be clear, I don't mean fucking everything that walks on two legs; I mean, monogamy is hard because people change. We're changing constantly, we're never really finished, yet we ask one person to try to keep adjusting, to love a dozen different variations of us. We pick our person and we try to make it work. Until it doesn't, maybe, but you make that choice and you play your hand till it runs out.

And then you meet some charming, handsome guy on vacation, he says.

You laugh, she says, but I'm serious. Being in touch with you makes me feel really guilty, sometimes. Because it's like I'm trying to have my cake and eat it, too, and that's not fair.

But everyone wants that.

Sure, she says, but only people who are assholes actually follow through.

I didn't know you felt this way, he says.

In all fairness, that's because I never told you.

Why didn't you?

Because it would have just made things messier.

So why are you telling me now?

Because for whatever reason, you do mean something to me, and maybe it's already a mess. She stops walking and turns to him. Whatever else it means, I wanted you to know it, and I guess I wanted to hear it back.

So. Now what?

I don't know about you, she says, but I could use a drink.

They find a place with picnic tables set up outside, and a band playing covers at a volume that still allows for room to talk. It feels less like a bar than a backyard where someone decided to serve drinks.

It's perfect, she declares.

With the weight of their earlier conversation lifted, the remaining hours of the day pass easily. They laugh and knock back a few cheap beers, and when the band gets lively and asks the crowd to get up off their asses, they grin at one another and take to the dirt. Around the time the sun begins to set, she says, I should probably hit the road.

They settle their tab and tip the band, and the short walk to the parking lot feels to both of them like it's over too soon. He reaches out as if to hug her, but she holds out her hand, keys still dangling.

You can't kiss me, she says.

Why would you say that?

Because I know you want to.

He starts to protest, but she gives him a look.

Seriously, he says, I won't.

You promise?

If I'd known there would be this much negotiation, I'd have just gone for a handshake.

Come here, she says.

He steps into her waiting arms and after a moment feels her body relax into his at the same time that she gives him a hard squeeze. Long seconds pass, and neither of them let go, and the smell of her shampoo is nearly enough to bring him to his knees.

He wants to say something worthy of the moment, but knows this is no time for words; they would only fuck it up. How many moments do we get like this one? A dozen, maybe, if we are lucky.

When she finally lets go, she gives him a long look.

Don't worry, he says, I'll see you soon.

I hope so.

***

III. 2021

She is busy scanning the departure monitors, and she almost misses him.

When she glances beside her, she experiences a glimmer of recognition that it takes her a moment to place. Vic, she says. The hair is a little longer than she remembers, but she is nearly certain it's him. She puts some bass in her voice this time, and when she calls his name again, he turns, sees her and lights up.

Oh my god, he says, what are the odds? Are you waiting on a connection?

Yep, she says. Heading home, actually. You?

Yeah, I got delayed so I've been wandering back and forth. The ghost of terminal B.

How much time do you have?

He glances at his watch.

At least enough for a drink.

So, how have you been? It feels like it's been a while, he says.

They are seated at one of the nameless bars between gates, each of them nursing a gin and tonic. A beer isn't strong enough to deal with the stress of the airport, she explains, and he orders the same.

I've been good. All things considered. Trying to get back to normal, you know?

I do, he says. This is my first time on the road in months. It's weird, but I think I kind of missed living out of a suitcase.

Oh no, I didn't. But it's nice to be doing something familiar.

I'll drink to that.

She gives him a look, gently shakes her head.

What?

I'm sorry, I just can't get over how long your hair is.

Yeah, I'm still getting used to it, he says, rubbing the back of his neck.

It looks good, she assures him.

I've missed you, he says. I'm sorry, I know we're usually not so nakedly emotional, but. You sort of disappeared on me last year. I wondered if, well, hell, it could have been a million things, right? And then we sat down and I noticed that ring on your finger, and I thought, oh. So that's where she went.

I'm sorry I didn't tell you, she says. She searches his face, but his expression is unreadable. I meant to. So many times, but I just kept putting it off, or I'd think of some reason not to. Are you angry? You're angry.

He waves the question away.

I get it, he says. I'd have probably done the same thing.

He smiles, but they both know it's just for show.

So, when is the wedding?

We don't have to talk about this.

Oh thank god, he says, and this time, the smile is genuine. I suppose congratulations are in order, though.

Only if you mean it, she says.

Come on, aren't we the sort of people who care about each other enough to lie?

Now it's her turn to smile.

Touché, she says.

Hey, he says. Do you ever wonder, if.

Yes, she says. All the time.

He nods, shakes the ice in the bottom of his glass.

Well, you should probably head out soon. You don't want to miss that plane.

Yeah, I guess you're right. She reaches for her purse, but he shakes his head.

I've got it, he says.

She stands up and he turns so that they are squared, shoulder to shoulder.

Will I see you again, she says.

I don't know. But I hope so.

She grabs his hand and he lets her, and for a moment, it's there on her face, all the things she won't say out loud.

I hope so, too, she says.

He thinks now would be a good time to say something clever, something for her to remember him by. Instead, he says, think of me once in a while, would you?

She smiles, and turns away before he can see the tears in her eyes. He watches until she blends into the crowd and is gone before turning back to order another drink.

THE GOD OF SMALL THINGS

I was there when you exchanged your first words,
during the first moment that you felt possibility
blossom. I was there when you first saw her face,
in the anticipation of your first kiss and in the
contentment of the moment after.

I was there when you fell in love: with a girl, a
song, a moment.

I came to you in the hours after your conflicts,
when you relinquished your anger and surrendered
to compassion. There was a part of me in every
silly nickname, every successful joke, every bout of
uncontrollable laughter.

I wriggled in your lover's toes when you
grabbed hold and spoke into the arch of her foot; I
rested in her hair when she laid her head in your lap
for the first time; I slept beside you as you read in the
night, turning pages delicately so as not to interrupt
the soft sound of her sleeping breath.

I was there in a cup of clam chowder, and a
splash of coke in a warm can, and in the pride you felt
when she laughed, and laughed, and laughed.

Each time she reached for you, I was there on
your wrist, in the spaces between your knuckles, in the
small of your back.

I was there in every photograph, and every
moment you reached out to take hold of before it
passed. I walked beside you in a life that you made,
inside a house that for a time, knew love.

You found traces of me still in each visit to
someplace else, your affection a uniquely portable
magic.

I was still there in the days when you did not
see me, when you wondered if I was one more thing

she had taken with her.

Look for me when you feel joy again, after believing, however briefly, that such things might be lost to you. I will be there in those moments that feel like a lightning strike, so bright and filled with hope; if you look closely, you will see me in every molecule.

I will be there when whole days pass before you remember that once you didn't think that you would ever feel this way again. I will be there when you find grace in moving your body the way it was meant to: forward, always forward.

Look for me in the resilience that follows your broken heart. Look for me in the face of every new lover, real or imagined; those faces that look upon yours with admiration, or wonder. Look for me when you no longer feel regret, but gratitude, for where you have been. Look for me when you are ready to begin living again, and I will be there, lingering in every crease and corner where you shine your light.

SIDE B

Where You've Been & Where You Want to Go

ENCHANTED ROCK

"We're lost, just admit it."

"We're not lost," he says, though he isn't entirely sure.

He would love to look at the map, but if he does that, he might never hear the end of it, and then it's all over.

"Didn't we just pass through this way? That tree looks familiar. I swear, if we're going in circles…"

They are not going in circles, per se. The irony that he is reluctant to point out, however, is that the trail they are on is a loop; an exceptionally long one, it turns out.

Yet another part of his rapidly crumbling plan was taking the Loop Trail, a nearly five mile jaunt that would show off the most beautiful features of the area and give each of them plenty of time to say whatever needed to be said. When he'd suggested the trip, his intention was to give them both some time away from work, from the city, from all the dozens of tiny things that were driving them apart.

On the ride over, a funny thing happened: the plan had worked, at least for a little while. They were getting along, singing and laughing together as she teased him about some of their disastrous attempts to go camping in the past.

"Babe, that's just some of the flora that's out here. We're moving in the right direction, I promise."

"Don't babe me right now. I'm not in the mood. And what are you, a botanist now?"

"You know, this was a spiritual place for several Native tribes. Maybe it's like The Twilight Zone," he suggests, humming the first few bars of the theme. "A place outside of space and time."

"That would explain why we've barely seen anyone else," she says.

It's not quite an olive branch, but her tone is softer.

"Or maybe we're the only people brave enough to start a hike in the middle of the day during a Texas summer," he says, putting on a country drawl.

This time she barks with laughter, a proper laugh, and he feels relieved.

"And by brave, of course, you mean dumb."

"Of course," he says.

"Seriously, Tom, check the map. I wanna know where we are."

"Okay."

Together, they unfold the pamphlet map and consult their location, determining that they have made it about half of the way around. She seems to be cooling off, so he decides not to play cheerleader. Maybe this difficulty will turn out to be a happy accident, the sort of thing that they will look back and laugh about together. Remember that time we almost got lost at that fucking rock? It's the kind of story you'd recount to your friends over drinks. We were so close to calling it, they'd say. The day or the relationship? Both! They would laugh. But being out there, something changed. Maybe there was something to the enchantment of the place after all.

***

Later, when they return to the campsite and get settled in, she comes to him, taking a seat beside him as he roots through his pack.

"What's up," he says.

"Tom, maybe we should have that talk now."

All at once, he knows what she will say: it's over. His last ditch effort was noble, but ultimately a waste. I'm sorry, he wants to tell her. I remember when things were good, and it still feels so much closer than it really is. I thought maybe if we both wanted it bad enough, we could get it back.

Instead, he says, "Sure. Maybe we could walk and talk?"

"Tom," she says.

"I know, I know. But we don't have to go far. Just wander out a little in the camping area. There's next to no light pollution out here, and it's supposed to be pretty amazing." He is sure that he has begun to sound desperate, but he smiles as if everything is fine.

"Okay," she says.

The temperature has cooled considerably now that the sun has gone, and they slip into thicker layers and lace up their boots, wandering back out into the desert, together for the last time. There are only a handful of people around, small pockets of friends and lovers huddling together or toying with mobile telescopes.

The night is even more beautiful than he might have hoped, the broad expanse of blue-black sky seeming to go on forever. The stars, seemingly infinite, glow in a way he has never seen before; he has never been somewhere so untouched by man. It is as if he could reach out and come away with stardust on his fingertips.

"You were right," she says. "It's incredible."

He can't quite make out her face in the dark, but it sounds as if there's tears in her voice.

"Sarah," he says.

"Wait, what's that?"

He looks up, and at first sees only more stars.

"What's what?"

"There," she says.

She moves closer to him, one hand on his arm while the other points to his right. Finally, he sees it: a star, he thinks, but one that is brighter than the rest. It's moving. Around them, some of the others are starting to notice as well, a collective buzz building among the campers.

"It's a falling star. Or maybe a comet? I've never actually seen one before."

"No," she says. "Look at the way it's moving. Really look."

He adjusts his eyes and sees what she means. The object—he has suddenly begun to think of it as an object—is moving in unusual patterns, at odd angles. It appears to be leaping, its movement almost balletic, and growing closer.

"That's definitely not a falling star," she says. "What the hell is it?"

A UFO, he almost says, but hesitates. Well, that's what it is, isn't it? He isn't saying it's a space man, per se, not a creature from another world, but it sure as hell doesn't move like anything he's ever seen.

"Maybe it's some kind of military craft," he says. "A training exercise for some advanced tech."

"I think it's E.T.," she says, her eyes tracking its movement.

It's in his nature to be skeptical, to prod and overthink things until he's picked them apart. He can feel himself gearing up to object, rational thought intruding on this moment he can't explain, but he hesitates. Isn't this what he wanted? Time, just a little bit more time before having to let go. Why not, he thinks. Why can't it be something extraordinary?

"Or maybe it's Ziggy Stardust," he says.

She laughs, and it is a giddy, ebullient sound. He can't remember the last time he made her laugh that way. Her hand slips from his arm and he feels himself wilt for a moment before she slips her fingers into his.

The object has grown closer, close enough that he can see the bright trail of light it leaves in its wake. For an instant, the object seems to pause in midair, and suddenly his vision is filled with light. He presses his eyes shut, his arm winding up like a shield.

When he opens them again, there is a kaleidoscope of colors dancing at the edge of his sight. He blinks them away, uncertain whether the world has become so much brighter, or if it was simply a refraction of that burst, whatever the hell it was.

Beside him, Sarah moves closer, not letting go of his hand.

"Oh, Tom," she says. "It's so beautiful. Maybe it's a sign."

"A sign of what?"

But she doesn't seem to hear him, or chooses not to answer. The people around them are jumping and yelling with excitement and can you believe it and what the hell was that.

No, it wasn't a sign, he thinks.

It's a second chance.

LIVING ROOM KARAOKE

The first time you hear about the karaoke apartment you are at work.

It's the middle of the week, and you are sitting at your desk, working on some mind numbing excel sheet, typing data sets in a distracted middle-of-the-afternoon haze.

You haven't been sleeping well, so at first you aren't sure if you're hearing it right. The man in the cubicle next to yours (his name starts with a D, you think) is speaking animatedly to a woman you vaguely recognize from accounting. It's this couple right, he is saying, and they have a karaoke bar in their living room. A whole bar? No, no, he says, it's an idiom.

You stop typing, certain that you must be misunderstanding, missing some vital piece of information.

Oh my god, that's wild, she is saying. Her excitement is unmissable. It will change your life, he tells her. You gotta go.

I'm sorry, you interrupt. I don't understand.

They both stop talking and look at you for a moment. You're not sure where this sudden boldness came from. You are not normally very outgoing, certainly not enough to disrupt a conversation between two coworkers you barely know.

What happens if these people aren't home, you continue. Or what if they want to go to sleep? The woman from accounting makes a face, as if to say she hadn't considered this. The man in the cubicle looks between you and says, it doesn't matter. That's ridiculous, you say. Instead of responding, the man simply shrugs and turns away.

***

Less than a week later, your sister asks you if you've heard
of this new karaoke bar. It's in someone's apartment,
she explains. It's the hot new place in town. You tell her
you haven't heard about it, vaguely embarrassed by your
behavior at work and therefore reluctant to explain how
you came by the knowledge. We should check it out this
weekend, she says.

Your sister is one of your closest friends. You are
three years younger and have always gotten along. When you
were growing up, she was always protective of you, made
sure that you were included in things, and whether it is out
of obligation or affection, she continues to do so now that
you are both adults. Okay, you say, that could be fun. I'll let
everyone know, she says, already reaching for her phone.

When the weekend comes around, you make plans to meet
in the parking lot, but an afternoon meeting runs long and
then you are stuck in traffic and are rushing to shower
and dress before the agreed upon time. You are only a few
minutes behind, but your sister texts you to say they are
heading inside and we'll see you soon, okay? You don't feel
particularly okay about it, but you'd rather not admit it, so
you say okay, great.

Eventually you arrive at a nondescript apartment
complex on the south side of town. There is a labyrinthine
parking structure that takes you up several levels, all of
which appear identical.

You make your way down to the first floor, looking
for unit 1576. There is nothing especially noteworthy about
this particular unit, at least from the outside. The door is
painted off white, a plain rubber welcome mat underneath.
You knock once, then again with a bit more force, but no one
answers.

After another minute, you try the door and find it

unlocked. You step into the apartment, unsure of whether you should call out.

Hello, you venture half-heartedly. You can hear the chatter of voices from beyond the foyer. There is a tall bookcase beside you, occupied by stacks of paperbacks with creased edges. The place is larger on the inside than you'd have guessed.

As you approach the living room, you see several people standing beside the breakfast bar. The apartment appears to be fully furnished; a couch and a loveseat, a sink full of dishes, a coffee table littered with magazines and mismatched coasters.

There is no sign of your sister or any of your friends. There is a tall woman with long dark hair shuffling in front of the TV, a chipped white coffee mug in her left hand. She is belting out the words to "Poker Face" but she must have lost her voice, because it comes out raspy and cracked. She doesn't seem to notice, or at least doesn't mind, because she appears to be enjoying herself. You wonder if she is just drunk.

There is a pair of stools at the bar so you take a seat and watch the performance for a moment before taking in the rest of the apartment. There is no evidence that the people who live here are bothered by the presence of what you can only assume are strangers. Hell, you think, maybe these *are* the people who live here.

You should take a turn, someone says. You crane your neck around to take in the tall woman with the raspy voice. What, you say, even though you heard her perfectly fine. You are trying to buy time, unsure of how to recuse yourself from having to sing. You're new here, I can tell. You should get up there. It will change your life, she says, echoing the colleague who's name you still cannot recall.

I don't know, you start to say. Come on, she offers, as if you'd agreed. I'll help you pick out a mic.

You get up and walk into the kitchen proper, hoping your sister will appear and give you an out, but she doesn't.

How about this, the woman asks, holding up a plastic bottle of cooking oil. You look around the kitchen and your eyes settle on a long wooden spoon. You have one just like it at home, you've used it to scramble eggs on occasion. I'll take this, you say, reaching for it and only then realizing that you have now committed to whatever bizarre ritual this woman expects you to perform.

Perfect, she says. Now you just have to pick a song.

The smart TV mounted on the wall is turned to the YouTube homepage. What do you want to sing, she asks. Um, you say. Do you know any Bowie? Sure, you say, I know Bowie. This is something of an understatement. You went through a Bowie phase in high school and you know most of his catalogue front to back. How about "Young Americans"?

The first notes of the song kick in and you're suddenly unsure of what to do. Where do my hands go, you wonder. How do I stand? Should I move? Is this spoon really meant to be a microphone?

You start softly when the first verse arrives, but your heart isn't in it. The other people must notice because it suddenly seems quieter. You start to feel panic rising in your chest. You got this, someone calls. The tall woman with the scratchy voice is shaking her hips in time to the music. She gives you a small nod of encouragement then goes back to dancing.

You close your eyes and start to two-step, tentatively at first, but before long you feel your body moving without needing to be told. You can feel yourself singing a little louder, a little louder, a little more sure of yourself. You may not be getting a record deal anytime soon, but you're not bad.

By the time the final minute of the song rolls around, you are lost to the music, having forgotten the strangers, the mysterious apartment, just where in the hell your sister went. There is just you and the music, and you feel good; you are in the zone, this must be what people mean when they say that and you get it now, you really get it.

Suddenly the song is over and you find that you are

sorry that it's ending. You clutch the spoon a little tighter. Wait, you want to say, I wasn't done.

You feel yourself sweating, a slight tingle running down your arms. Oh my god, you hear a familiar voice say, a hand on your shoulder. That was amazing! You turn, expecting to see the tall girl again, but it's your sister. I can't believe you did that, she says. You were amazing! How do you feel?

You want to tell her how alive you felt, like there was electricity coursing through your blood. You want to tell her that you weren't afraid. For a moment, it felt like you were in control. Is this how people feel all the time, you want to ask. The rest of your friends appear and as someone hugs you, you try to catch your sister's eye.

I feel good, you say.

I feel so fucking good.

CLOAK AND DAGGER

We take technology for granted now.

That's not meant to be news to anyone, but when was the last time you considered how remarkable our lives have become? If you're of a certain age, you may remember a time before we were always so connected.

We used to memorize home phone numbers, navigating hostile older siblings or chatty parents, each call a potential negotiation with the unknown. Making plans was an art form; if you missed your ride, you'd have to hope you knew where to go (and had another way of getting there) or risk missing out. Birthdays were something you likewise committed to memory or otherwise relied upon your parents for, particularly when it came time to visit a distant cousin or sign a card for your favorite uncle.

When I was a teenager, cell phones were in their nascent stages. I can still remember a time in my life before I began to rely on having one; late nights spent whispering in hushed tones on your cordless line, determined to beat the shrill ring before it woke everyone in the house.

Thinking back, it amazes me how rich our young lives must have felt, bursting with enough drama and hunger to fuel all-night sessions, each of us so eager to be understood. Even when you weren't serenading some member of the opposite sex, there was a clandestine quality to these calls, a teenage version of cloak and dagger.

Among my friends, there was a girl (as if there was anything else for a teenage boy). Her name was Katherine, but only her mother and our teachers called her that. To the rest of us, she was just Kat.

Even among our tight-knit group, we were a pair; in the right company, I wouldn't have hesitated to admit she was my best friend. Or at least, this is how I remember it.

***

It had been years since I had thought of her, or the person that I was then. I was not an especially unpopular child, but I was often very unhappy for reasons that remain unclear to me even now. When I recount those days, I always chalk it up to hormones, but the truth, I believe, is that the growing pains of adolescence simply magnified an innate sadness that was already there, lying in wait. Count me among those who left the proverbial teenage wasteland and never thought to look back.

After my parents sold my childhood home, my mother asked me to go through a few boxes of things she believed to be mine. I spent an unremarkable Saturday afternoon in our half-finished basement casually leafing through old yearbooks and misbegotten poetry before relegating most of the contents to the trash.

Buried among the rubble, however, was a photo album which I recognized as dating back to the summer before I entered high school. There were several group photos which included Kat, but the one that caught my attention was of just the two of us, impossibly young, our eyes vaguely red from the flash. I am facing the camera, but Kat is looking at me coolly, her arm draped across my shoulder. It's the sort of look that would have resulted in merciless teasing had the roles been reversed, but none of our friends would have made those kinds of jokes at her expense.

It was only after I brought the album into my apartment that it occured to me that I had no real clue what had become of her. I checked all the usual places, but she turned up on no social media sites. I had no email address, no phone number, no leads at all. Her absence from our ubiquitous digital life led some small part of me to doubt that she had ever existed. It's ridiculous, I know, but there's something sort of unreal about someone who can't be found at the click of a few buttons, isn't there?

For the next several weeks, I was consumed by my curiosity. It became a need that I began to feel rattling in the back of my teeth.

I reached out to a few friends, trying to lean into my inquiry casually, realizing how strange it must have sounded. No one could say anything for certain. Someone said they believed she'd gotten married and moved out west. Couldn't say for sure, but hey man, how have you been? How about them Birds?

Memory can be fickle, and even cruel. We often choose to remember the things that suit us and cast aside the rest. But here is what I believe to be honest and objectively true: Kat was a girl of above average height, with short raven-black hair. She had large, expressive eyes and full lips. She had a deep voice, and a throaty laugh, a combination that always made her seem older somehow. She was fiercely loyal and unusually self-possessed, already so much more at ease with her identity than the rest of us.

I wish I could say more with certainty, to draw in those lines that would make her more real. I remember Kat only in sketches; fragments, and feelings that are just this side of surety. At some point, clearly, we lost touch. There may have been a falling out, but who can say? We might just as easily have drifted apart, the way so many of us did in those days.

Before they left for good, I called my mother to ask if there were any more boxes that she might have missed, hoping for something that might hold some clue as to what had happened. No, there was nothing else. Sorry honey, but your father and I would love to have you over for dinner at the new house when you have time.

In the days before the internet, it was entirely possible to never see a person again and to know nothing of what became of them, except to wonder. So I have: I've wondered with an unusual intensity about whether she found someone, or had children; whether she loves her career, if she's still close to her mother, or if she was ever able to forgive her father for leaving.

Briefly, I considered hiring a PI before I realized how utterly insane it sounded. Hello, yes, I'd like you to find a missing person. When was the last time I saw her? Oh, going on twenty plus years now. You see, she's not missing per se, at least not that I know of. You see, it's just that I don't know how to reach her any longer, and I've been seized by this irrational need to know what she's up to.

Eventually, more practical concerns emerged. Even if I did find her, what could I possibly have to say that would justify going through the trouble? Hi, do you remember me, your friend from years ago? What have you done with your life, who have you become? Do you also remember those days? Do you share any curiosity about what became of me?

It's impossible, perhaps even reckless of me to say no, but I suppose I'll say it anyhow. Someone who has so thoroughly evaded modernity surely has no need for a half-remembered past. No, someone like that lives in the present; a feat which I admit did not come easily to me even before we possessed the ability to always be somewhere else.

I've always believed nostalgia is for suckers; stay too long in the past, that refuge of the hopeless and the forgotten, and you can poison your present. Yet sometimes, when I am sad or bored, I still find myself returning to that photo album, marveling at who we used to be.

If I am honest (and really, there isn't much point to this otherwise) I have looked for her in part because I crave validation; the kind that might have once sustained a lonely young man, to know that what he felt was real, and that it happened. I realized how badly what I wanted was simply to show her that photo of the two of us and say hey, look, there we are.

***

The last memory I have of her takes place on a summer night at the house I grew up in.

It is just the two of us; I cannot recall how it came to be this way, just that she cannot stay for long. I don't remember what we might have said, but I do remember the feeling of her hand in mine, and the fleeting warmth of her lips as they grazed my cheek. Was it a declaration of love, or perhaps a goodbye? It might have been neither, since I can't say for certain that this was the last time we ever saw one another. Our minds, though, are built to make sense of our disparate memories, and this seems as good a place to end as any.

Does she remember this moment as well, wherever she may be? Is it different from the other side of the fence? Surely, it must be. What it might mean to her, I am sure I will never know, and maybe that's for the best. The truth may set you free, but it will just as often leave you hopelessly disappointed, as well.

People tend to crave closure, and I used to be one of them, but I'm not so sure anymore. What's more beautiful than a riddle that you can grow alongside of? The circle never closes, the romance never grows stale, and the answer is always whatever you need it to be.

In an age where there are so few mysteries left; Kat, my old friend, remains maddeningly, beautifully, perfectly out of reach.

HAUNTED

They went to the carnival every year.

It had been a tradition since they were boys, taking to their bicycles and riding through the valley, seizing the freedom they were blessed with on those cool autumn nights.

As those boys grew into young men, they traded in their bikes, instead piling into cars with girls, passing around warm beer acquired in secret, and in this way they tasted their future.

One day adulthood took root, sending them off to full-time work, college, or some other far-flung adventure. Some of them left the valley and did not return, but those who were of a mind did so every October as long as they were able.

They returned even when it had been many years since any of them had felt excitement about funnel cakes or Ferris wheels, because it kept them anchored to the place they had once called home; it connected them to friends who had known them before life had taught them how to be someone else.

They exchange greetings like hey brother, it's great to see you. You're looking trim, you've been working out? Me, I'm working on filling this belly out. How's the job, the girl, your folks, the kids?

The carnival itself is bright with halogen and neon, a cacophony of sounds: men shout over the whir of machinery, children scream in delight or terror, the distant hum of a calliope echoes.

It's a small town, and sometimes they bump into former teachers or neighbors, old classmates who never left town, many of whom are surprised to see their youthful tradition remains unbroken.

Though few of them might think to say it aloud,

it's the unchanging familiarity of this place that comforts them; the belief that yeah, maybe you can go home again.

The group drifts through the grounds, in no particular hurry, and with no particular destination. It has been years since any of them has taken to a ride, though a few beers will often bring out someone's competitive side, laughing and shit-talking at the ring toss like they are kids again.

Twenty years is a long time, but for many of those years, they have seen the same faces running the rides and manning the booths, career travelers without families or a need to call one place home. The boys remember some of them, greet them as if they are seeing old friends, make up stories about who these people are when the lights go down and the tents are packed up.

Many of the same staple attractions have remained too, the carnival not being an especially progressive or financially solvent industry. There are not often many new things, so this year they are quick to notice the shoddy trailer that they agree is one they've never seen before. What strikes them as unusual is the total lack of branding: there are no signs, no lights, no images at all beyond a few words hastily written above the entrance in what appears to be white paint: ENTER IF YOU DARE. Even the barker outside, a tall, vaguely haggard man with heavy lidded eyes, barely calls out or even seems to pay them any mind.

Hey man, someone says. What's the deal, is this like a haunted house?

Ah, gentleman, the man says, it is, but not just any haunted house.

He has suddenly come alive, his long arms gesturing with practiced animation, like a spider constructing a web. It's a personalized experience. You see, this place has special properties. The boys smile at one another. The old man is a natural. It's capable of shapeshifting, if you will. It can see inside your heart and know your true self.

So what's the scary part, someone jokes. That's pretty high concept for a traveling carnival, someone else says.

Yeah, pretty avant-garde, a third chimes in.

They thank the old man for the show and go to move on, but one of them stays behind.

Yo, J, you coming?

Actually, I think I wanna check it out, he says.

Really? His friends laugh. Since when do you like haunted houses?

He shrugs. I dunno, it sounds kind of interesting.

Hell, one of the others says, I'll come with you. Why not?

The old man raises a hand.

It's best if you go one at a time, he says.

Is that part of the pitch? Divide and conquer?

They laugh, but the old man says nothing.

Okay, right on, old timer. J, I guess you're on your own, man.

See you on the other side, fellas, he says and then steps up to the door.

Once inside, it's as if he's stepped into a vacuum, so suddenly are the myriad of lights and sounds almost completely gone. They must have soundproofed the place, he thinks, knocking gently on the wall. Is that standard? He isn't sure, but it's effective.

The first room is ordinary by haunted house standards, replete with eerie music, plastic knives hanging from the ceiling, cheap scenes of Halloween store carnage. As he moves through the next several rooms, it is largely more of the same: a zombie-filled graveyard, then witches conspiring around a large cauldron, flashing strobe lights and paper-mache flying saucers.

He takes a sharp left, expecting to see the familiar neon EXIT sign overhead, but he doesn't.

Instead, he finds himself at the mouth of a short, empty hallway, which leads to a plain, metallic door. He glances back, curious if he missed a cue somehow, if he's taken a wrong turn and ended up behind the scenes.

As he makes his way down the hall, a door slams

behind him, effectively pinning him in. This sudden escalation is the first thing that's actually thrown him off balance. He grins nervously, the jolt of fear also a bit of a thrill.

When he reaches the other end, he leans into the spring loaded push bar (for a split second, expecting it not to move) and then he is through to the next room, a space the size of a small living room, with long paneled mirrors on three sides.

The sound of his laughter is both pleasure and release, nerves evaporating. I'm surprised it wasn't clowns, he thinks.

Without warning, the lights go down, and images begin spilling soundlessly out of the mirrors.

No, not *out* of them, exactly, but as they spread from one panel to the next, the effect becomes disorienting as they begin to overlap, all but surrounding him. He looks around, searching for some kind of projector, but sees nothing in the dim light.

It is because he is distracted that he doesn't immediately realize what he is seeing are images of himself. He is much younger in some of the scenes that flicker past, but as he regains his focus, he is increasingly sure what he is seeing is his own life, reflected back at him somehow.

Okay, what the fuck? He says aloud. How are you doing this?

The images begin to flash more quickly, and all he can think of is the manic way in which calliope music picks up speed, going round and round until it reaches a fever pitch.

He suddenly feels nauseous, overrun by a strong urge to look away. I'm not afraid, he wants to say, but I don't like this and I would very much like it to end now, please. You got me, you creepy carny fuck. I don't know how you're doing this, but you got me.

He closes his eyes.

As abruptly as the images began, they are suddenly gone.

In their place is the image of a boy, nearly a young

man. There is a filmy quality to the boy, as if the image is being projected from further away.

He takes a step forward, then another one, stopping short of coming close enough to touch the glass.

What, he says. Are you real?

The boy does not answer, but when he blinks, the lights flutter, and the boy is gone, but only for a moment. He blinks again, and sees the boy once more, his hand extended as if he means to show him something.

What the hell is this, he says.

The boy continues to regard him silently, his hand outstretched.

I'm scared, he finally says. I guess I have been for a long time. But you already knew that. Didn't you?

Okay, he says, reaching out toward the glass.

Okay.

***

Whoa, there he is, his friends say when he returns. The tall man is gone, replaced by a bored middle aged woman who regards them with a similar air of indifference.

How was it, they ask. Did it work?

Were you spooked?

Thinking of Ray Bradbury

LAST RIDE OF THE SEASON

You decide it's now or never.

Tomorrow, you will be getting on a plane and returning home, to the person you already are there. Today, though, there is still time for you to be anything. Today, you will be the kind of person who conquers your fears.

It has been almost two months since you last spoke to her, a bit longer since you last saw her face. Already, you have forgotten the sound of her voice, the way she laughed, the way she said your name. You came here to forget, or if not to forget, to put some distance between you and your pain.

You have been lonely here, too, but the air is cleaner, almost sweet, and it has a calming effect. The speed of your thoughts, so often like a runaway train, slow down long enough for you to watch them go by. You try to let them, without looking too long or passing undue judgement.

You stand watching from the dirt path as the gondola cars pass by, slowing long enough to gather passengers, then drifting up the mountain toward somewhere else.

Now or never, you say aloud, as if it's a spell that will compel you to move. When the next car drifts by, you climb in and close the door before you have a chance to think.

As the car begins to rise, the foliage grows more densely packed. You are surrounded by not much more than trees beginning to shed for winter, and a few clouds that feel close enough to touch.

You don't like heights, you never have. You try not to look behind you, but of course you do, and the effect is dizzying.

The town grows smaller and smaller, but the mountain ahead of you is unchanging in its majesty. It reminds you of how small you are, how ephemeral. You think this should make you sad, but it doesn't. Instead, you feel grateful. It is a reminder of time passing, of things that are constant and things that are not.

You will feel love again, and in turn, you will know what it is to be loved. This is not the first, nor will it be the last (no, far from it) of your heartbreak, but this time will always remain singular.

You will not understand why for a long time; it will be years before you will think to trace back the path that began when you got on that plane by yourself, determined to survive the fear of being alone, to quiet the nagging voice at the back of your mind that tells you that you won't get another chance.

Years from now, the woman whom you came here to forget will have married someone else. You will think of her from time to time, even dream of her, and wonder at what might have been. We were so young, you will think, with both compassion and a hint of regret.

Near the top of the mountain, you can see into the valley below, the sun just beginning to set on the resort on the other side, casting everything you can see into vibrant shades of gold and green.

There are a few precious seconds left before the car will begin its descent, and you feel the panic flutter in your chest as you try to hold onto this moment, this feeling.

You do not realize it now, but this car is a chrysalis, delivering you to someplace new.

You look back, and for a single moment, you are perfectly balanced. You wish you could stay here just a little longer, suspended between here and there, but you know better.

As the car lurches forward and begins the trip back down, you close your eyes, sit back, and enjoy what's left of the ride.

ACKNOWLEDGEMENTS

First, thanks to my mom, who has always been my biggest fan and who gifted me with my love of reading and then championed my love of writing. And to my father—to paraphrase from the man who said it best—when I was a teenager, he was so ignorant, I could hardly stand to have him around, but when I hit my 20s, I was astonished at how much the old man had learned in a few short years.

Many thanks to my early readers, in particular to M., who provided inspiration, and after only a bit of cajoling, invaluable feedback as well.

I owe a great debt to the teachers who nurtured my love of reading and the ones who encouraged me to keep writing. Special thanks to Tara, Sarah and Alicia who managed this feat during my teenage years, when I was undoubtedly at my most insufferable.

Thanks, too, to my extended family; both the Kinsleys and the Dabieros and everyone who has joined our merry band of misfits over the years. I'm grateful for every one of you, and in particular Debbie (who never let up on asking me when I would write more), Peggy (for always having a great book recommendation at the ready) and Michael, who always found a way to make me feel like the Man. Lastly, to the memory of Evelyn Dabiero, who was one of the most wonderful people I've ever known. She made a lot of lives significantly brighter, but especially mine.

A special shout out to François, a great writing partner, editor, and friend. I haven't written anything he didn't have his fingerprints on in the last five years, and the work is always better after he's given his blessing.

This book is dedicated to the Gypsy Soul gang, without whom I am confident these stories wouldn't exist. When I needed it most, you all made me laugh, made me feel worthy, and reminded me of the unexpected and extraordinary ways that life goes on. Thanks again to Tara, Megan, Ruby, Jordan, and most of all, my brother Nick, who has always encouraged and inspired me to keep creating. I hope we get to have many, many more days like the one on the river.

I've been incredibly fortunate to have people who believed in me at every stage of my life (you know who you are) and if you're still here, thank you, thank you, thank you. I've always wanted to be a writer, which is to say, I've always wanted to write a book. Whatever happens next, this experience will rank among the greatest privileges and pleasures of my life.

Finally, dear reader, thanks to you for allowing me the opportunity to share this with you. I hope if you've made it this far, you found something worth spending your time and money on.

These stories belong to you now, too.